Darby
THE LOST AND FOUND PUPPY

Written by
Laura Rossiter

Illustrated by
Pat Whittaker

Laura was going on an airplane to visit her Grandmother in Minnesota, and she was bursting with excitement. She was even more excited because her new puppy, Darby, was taking the trip too.

After saying goodbye to her parents, Laura had a talk with Darby.

"I wish you could sit next to me," said Laura, "but you have to take this trip in your crate." Darby just licked Laura's face—she wanted to play. But now it was time for Laura to get on the plane with the other passengers.

"You'll only be alone for a little bit, I promise," said Laura, giving her puppy one last hug. "Once we get to Minnesota, Grammy and I will come to get you. And then we'll get to play in the snow!"

Laura helped Darby into her crate, and then she went to get on the airplane. Sadly, Darby rested her head on her favorite squeaky toy.

As Laura climbed the stairs to the plane, she didn't notice where Darby's crate was being loaded. It was going on the wrong airplane!

The airplane was loud, but Darby fell fast asleep. When she woke up, the plane had already landed. Now she was in a big room surrounded by boxes and other crates, waiting for Laura.

A man who worked at the airport noticed Darby as he was checking the other boxes and crates.

"Hey there," he said, kneeling down. "Mmm. Looks like you were put on the wrong flight. You got sent to Texas, little puppy. That's a long way from Minnesota."

Darby didn't understand, but she was starting to get worried. Where was Laura? Why wasn't she here?

Darby couldn't stand it any longer. As soon as the man left, she nudged the crate door with her nose. To her surprise, the door popped open! She was free!

Darby walked around until she saw some light coming from a door. At the entrance, she let her soft coat be warmed in the sunshine. Poor Darby! She was supposed to be in Minnesota, playing with Laura in the snow! And here she was, alone and lost in Texas.

But Darby didn't know that as she walked off in search of Laura.

Little Darby soon found herself in the middle of a busy airport!

Airplanes were taking off and landing. Engines roared. Tires screeched.

"Get that dog off the runway!" a man shouted. Darby looked up and saw an airplane heading right in her direction.

Terrified, she sped across the hot pavement as fast as her paws could go. Spotting a small hole in a fence, she ran to it and squeezed herself through to the other side.

It was another hectic place—a construction
site, with men, machines and a giant hole in the
ground.

"Hey, I wonder what that puppy's doing way
out here?" said a worker.

"She's got a collar," another man said. "So she must belong to someone. Let's get her some water, then try to find her owner."

Before she knew it, Darby was swept up in the strong arms of a construction worker and placed carefully in the front seat of a pickup truck. She even got to wear a hard hat! Away she went, past loaders, bulldozers and dump trucks.

The construction workers took Darby to a nearby coffee shop where the waitress gave her a
cool bowl of water. Everyone made a fuss over
the little lost puppy.

As she drank from the bowl, Darby looked
outside. Suddenly, a little girl walked past. Was
that Laura? Just then the coffee shop door
swung open. Darby barked twice and quickly
scampered out after the little girl.

Darby followed the little girl into a nearby store. "Ruff! Ruff!" Darby barked, in her loudest happy puppy bark.

But when the girl turned around, Darby's heart sank. It wasn't Laura after all.

"Look Daddy!" said the little girl. "It's a puppy! Oh Daddy, can we keep her?"

"Well honey," said the tall man, "this pup's got a collar and a tag. It says her name is Darby. My goodness, pup, you're a long way from home!"

"But Daddy, she's all alone!" cried the little girl.

"I'll tell you what," answered her father. "We'll take her back to the ranch and try to call her owners. How about that?"

Darby soon found herself on one of
the biggest ranches in Texas.

"Look, Darby!" said the little girl. "I'll bet
you've never seen real cowboys before."

What a sight! Cowboys, cattle and horses.
Darby even got to wear a real cowboy hat!

She was having a wonderful time, but she still
missed Laura. Darby yawned. She was getting
tired too.

Using the information on Darby's collar, the rancher called Laura's father and found out how the puppy got to Texas.

"I'll make sure she's on the right plane this time," joked the rancher, who agreed to get Darby on the next plane to Minnesota.

Back at the airport, Darby's tail wagged as she once again crawled into the crate that still held her blanket and squeaky toy.

"I'll miss you, little Darby," whispered the girl.

Soon Darby was on another airplane, flying to meet Laura.

After the long flight from Texas, Darby's crate was carried into the airport in Minnesota.

"Darby! Darby!" Laura called as she ran toward her puppy.

The second her crate was opened, Darby leapt into Laura's arms.

"Oh, Darby, I missed you!" Laura said while hugging her puppy.

Darby wagged her tail so fast that her whole body wiggled with joy. She wasn't a lost puppy anymore. She was found!